NO LONGER PROPERTY OF
SEATTLE PUBLIC LIBRARY

D0531714

For all the brave kids who have done
what they once thought undoable —A.C.

Farrar Straus Giroux Books for Young Readers
An imprint of Macmillan Publishing Group, LLC
120 Broadway, New York, NY 10271

Copyright © 2020 by Aidan Cassie
All rights reserved
Color separations by Embassy Graphics
Printed in China by Toppan Leefung Printing Ltd., Dongguan City, Guangdong Province
Designed by Cassie Gonzales

Esperanto translations by Thomas "Tomaso" Alexander

First edition, 2020

1 3 5 7 9 10 8 6 4 2
mackids.com

Library of Congress Control Number: 2019948803
ISBN 978-0-374-31046-2

Our books may be purchased in bulk for promotional, educational, or business use. Please
contact your local bookseller or the Macmillan Corporate and Premium Sales Department
at (800) 221-7945 ext. 5442 or by email at MacmillanSpecialMarkets@macmillan.com.

THE WORD FOR FRIEND

AIDAN CASSIE

FARRAR STRAUS GIROUX
NEW YORK

From her new house, Kemala could see her new town. Somewhere in her new town was her new school. It was filled with new friends.

She was sure of it.

At the new market, Kemala helped her mama shop for school supplies. Everything was wonderfully unusual in her new country. Kemala told her mama each thing that was different.

Kemala *loved* talking.

The kids at her new school liked talking, too. But their words were different. They spoke a language Kemala didn't know.

"Do they speak *our* language?" she asked her mama.

"No," Mama whispered, "but we'll catch on."

When her mama left, the teacher spoke Kemala's name in a friendly voice. Kemala was shy at first, but soon she was telling the class all about herself. It took two and a half minutes.

When she was done, the room was quiet. Some kids giggled. No one had understood her words.

Kemala's tummy went all fluttery.

She curled into a ball and pretended she was alone.

Later, the other kids played leapfrog . . .

. . . cut out fancy hats . . .

. . . and sang a frog-counting song.

Kemala did not leap. Or cut. Or sing.

She stayed in a ball. All her wonderful words were missing.

After what felt like forever,
it was finally time for recess.

High in the branches, Kemala cut leaves into animal shapes. She was good at cutting. But she was absolutely *not* good at speaking a whole new language.

An anteater from her class popped down, pointed to herself, and said some words Kemala didn't know.

Mia nomo estas Ana!

She guessed the anteater's name must be Ana.

Kemala showed Ana how to cut the leaves with her sharp claws. Ana really liked cutting, too . . .

. . . even though she made a mess of it.

At circle time, Ana proudly held up one of her shredded leaves.

The room was quiet again. Some kids chuckled at her *hipopotamo*. Kemala imagined it was supposed to be a hippopotamus. Ana laughed the hardest.

When Mama picked her up from school, Kemala started talking like she'd been holding her breath all day.

"Mama! The school has a giant maple tree and the rug has soft cushions and we made frog hats and the kids are nice even though some have big teeth and the teacher told me *verda* means 'green,' but, Mama—

"I think we should go back home," said Kemala. "They don't know I like acting and drawing and eating termite jelly. I'll never learn *all* the words. I just CAN'T!"

Mama gave her a big hug.

Kemala didn't want to go to school the next day, but at recess she found Ana up in the big maple. Ana had brought thick black paper. Together they cut and cut.

El -eph...

Elefanto

Kemala cut out the shapes of friends she used to know:
a binturong, an orangutan, and a mouse-deer. Using twigs
and sap, she made them into delicate stick puppets.

Ana made a sloth . . . kind of.

As Kemala made an elephant, she felt Ana watching how
she carefully turned the paper and attached the tiny limbs.

The following week, Ana came to school with a bundle of puppets she'd worked on at home. They were far better than her first ones—some were fancy and some were plain, but all were fantastic to Kemala.

Kemala and Ana
used them to tell
each other stories.

Kemala's were
silent, but she
loved making the
puppets act.

And though Kemala
understood only some
of Ana's words, she
loved hearing them all.

One day Ana brought Kemala a special puppet
she'd made as a gift: a magnificent tiger with
intricate, cut-out stripes and carefully hinged legs.

Kemala wanted to say how much she loved the puppet. It reminded her of a story from her homeland where a clever mouse-deer outwits a silly tiger. Kemala knew Ana would like the story, but she didn't have the right words to tell it. That's when she had an idea.

Maybe she didn't have *all* the words, but Kemala couldn't wait to speak any longer. In her new language, she said . . .

Venu. Spektaklon. Vidu. Belaj patroj.
Ne, ne— belaj *pupoj*!
La granda arbo. Ĉi- nokte.
Mi kaj Ana, mia amiko!

"Come. A show. See. Beautiful fathers.
No, no—beautiful *puppets*!
The big tree. Tonight.
Me and Ana, my friend!"

The room was quiet.

Kemala knew she'd made a mess of it. Then everyone cheered. No one seemed to care about her mistakes at all.

That evening, Ana hung a sheet for a screen, and Kemala brought lights and a lantern. Together they put on a grand shadow-puppet show.

The audience laughed when Ana's mouse-deer tricked a hungry tiger into eating pudding made of mud. They applauded when Kemala's tiger got caught by the cobra, who wasn't a belt after all. And though her actions did most of the talking that night, Kemala tried more and more words every day.

Kemala had always loved talking, but most of all . . .

Ni vidu kiu havas la pli longan...

Miaj malnovaj amikoj mankas al mi, sed mi, Sed ĉu formikoj iam

Tigro estas belaj.

Ĉu vi havas genfratojn? Mi havas neniujn, Ellogigi el mia hejmo estis malfacile.

Mi volas ludi instrumenton kiam mi estos plenkreska. La

lang...
mi tre gojas,...
provas eniri viajn orelojn? Mi... Ĉu vi...
Mi ŝatas bani min en koto. Ĉu vi...
Mi satas ilin. Krom kiam ili estas malĝojaj...
Mia familio mankas al mi. Mi esperas, ke ni revenos...
sed foje mi kaj mia patrino kverelas.
sono de violono plaĉas al mi, sed mi kredas, ke miaj bra...
Miaj skvamoj estas et la sama material...

She loved making a new *amiko*, friend.

The Second Language

Kemala's new language in this book is Esperanto. Esperanto was created in 1887 by L. L. Zamenhof to provide the world with an easy-to-learn common language. Today it has about two million speakers worldwide. Because it is not associated with any particular country, it was chosen to make Kemala's new home feel like it could be anywhere, while probably feeling like a foreign language to most readers.

Esperanto translations

Welcome, Kemala. Bonvenon, Kemala.

So, what did you do? Do, kion vi faris?

I had to jump! Mi devis salti!

That's why I don't climb trees. Tial mi ne grimpas arbojn.

Make it taller. Plialtigu ĝin.

You can have it. Vi povas havi ĝin.

It's so beautiful! Ĝi estas tiel bela!

My name is Ana! Mia nomo estas Ana!

It's a hippo! Ĝi estas hipopotamo!

I miss my old friends, but I'm so glad I found you. Miaj malnovaj amikoj mankas al mi, sed mi tre ĝojas, ke mi trovis vin.

We should see who has a longer tongue. Ni vidu kiu havas la pli longan langon.

I like to take mud baths. Mi ŝatas bani min en koto.

My scales are made out of the same thing as my nails. Miaj skvamoj estas el la sama materialo kiel miaj ungoj.

PANGOLINS

There are eight different pangolin species living in Asia and Africa. Because some people value their scales and meat, all are threatened with extinction.

A pangolin can eat more than seventy million ants every year!

Pangolins have no teeth; the ants they eat are ground up by spines in their stomachs along with the help of stones they swallow.

Pangolins are the only mammals covered in scales. Their scales are made of keratin, just like rhino horns and our fingernails.

The closest relatives of pangolins are carnivores, like wolves and bears, even though they look and act a lot like anteaters.

Baby pangolins ride on their mothers' tails!

When pangolins are afraid, they protect themselves by curling up in a tight ball.